MW00982342

# FUNNY BOY TAKES ON THE CHITCHATTING CHEESES FROM CHATTANOOGA

# Dan Gutman

## Illustrated by Mike Dietz

OPEN ROAD
INTEGRATED MEDIA

All rights reserved under International and Pan-American Copyright Conventions. By payment of the required fees, you have been granted the non-exclusive, non-transferable right to access and read the text of this book. No part of this text may be reproduced, transmitted, downloaded, decompiled, reverse engineered, or stored in or introduced into any information storage and retrieval system, in any form or by any means, whether electronic or mechanical, now known or hereinafter invented, without the express written permission of the publisher.

This is a work of fiction. Names, characters, places, and incidents either are the product of the author's imagination or are used fictitiously. Any resemblance to actual persons, living or dead, businesses, companies, events, or locales is entirely coincidental.

Copyright © 2000 by Dan Gutman
Interior illustrations © 2000 by Mike Dietz
Cover illustration © 2012 by Mike Dietz

cover design by Mimi Bark

ISBN 978-1-4532-9530-4

This edition published in 2012 by Open Road Integrated Media
180 Varick Street
New York, NY 10014
www.openroadmedia.com

*Dedicated to George Crum,*
*the inventor of the potato chip.*

*Look it up if you don't believe me.*

NOTE TO READER: If you are looking for a well-written, educational book with a deep and positive message that will impress your parents and teacher with how smart you are, guess what? You picked the wrong book! Ha-ha-ha-ha!

This book is for laughs. If there is anything in this book that you find personally offensive, consult your doctor immediately and ask about getting a sense of humor transplant.

The story you are about to read has been carefully screened by the Parents Advisory Board to be certain it has no words such as dork, booger, moron, or armpit. If you see any words like those, alert the authorities.

# INTRODUCTION

*AH, HAHAHAHAHAHAHAHAHA!*

Thought you'd gotten rid of me, didn't you? Nice try! Well, I'm back, and funnier than ever!

I am Funny Boy, defender of all that is evil and enemy to all that is good. Oops, I mean the other way around! I have been sent here to save Earth from the unspeakably disgusting aliens that have been landing and inhabiting your planet right under your very noses.

Wake up, Earth people! While you sleep, go to school, and watch television, alien sleazeballs are threatening your way of life. It is up to me, and only me, to defend your planet from the forces of evil and wickedness wherever I might find them. My weapons: jokes, puns, quips, wisecracks, and sometimes . . . if necessary . . . toilet humor.

You probably think I'm crazy. Fine. But keep this in mind: In Funny Boy #1, I used my superior sense of humor to save Earth from the airsick alien from Andromeda. In Funny Boy #2, I used my superior sense of humor to save Earth from the bubble-brained barbers from the Big Bang.

Do you still doubt that aliens are in your midst? And can you continue to doubt the power of my sense of humor?

This is no joke, Earth people. Something very curious occurred to me after I drove off those bubble-brained barbers. Not only were aliens attacking Earth, I realized, but they were attacking ... in alphabetical order!

If my theory is correct, the next alien force will start with the letter C. It could be alien communists, or alien cartoonists. Alien condominiums or alien contact lenses. I have to watch for the letter C *very* carefully.

I know what you're thinking. If Funny Boy truly saved Earth twice, how come you didn't hear about it on the news? How come nobody brought a current events report about it to school?

Well, I'll tell you why. There's a massive government cover-up going on. You see, your government is so petrified that people will panic, they invent ridiculous stories so the public won't know about alien invasions.

You know those Tickle Me Elmo dolls that were so popular for a while? You probably thought they were just adorable talking toys. Well, think again. Millions of those things were programmed to blow up the first time they were tickled on Christmas morning. But thanks to me, it didn't happen.

That's okay, you don't have to thank me now. I was just doing my job. The satisfaction of having saved the planet is enough reward for me.

Just to let you know, I've got my eye on this Harry Potter kid, too. I don't trust him.

I can prove to you that there's a government cover-up aimed at preventing the general public from finding out about all the alien attacks on Earth. Just the other day I was watching the news and they were talking about a meteor shower that people would be able to see that night.

Ha! I knew perfectly well that meteors don't *take* showers. In fact, they hardly bathe at all. That meteor shower was an invasion by some very evil aliens who wanted to turn your entire state of Nevada into a desert. Lucky for you, I was around to stop them.

So if you want to know the truth about what's going on up in the sky at night, listen to me. Believe me, brother, it's scary out there. If you think that airsick alien and those bubble-brained barbers were tough, wait until you read about the intergalactic dirtball I had to do battle with this time. . . .

**—FUNNY BOY**

# CHAPTER 1

# WHICH YOU DON'T HAVE TO READ IF YOU ALREADY READ THE FIRST TWO FUNNY BOY BOOKS, BUT YOU CAN IF YOU FEEL LIKE IT, OR HAVE NOTHING BETTER TO DO WITH YOUR LIFE.

*Why was 6 afraid of 7?*

*Because 7 8 9.*

That was one of the first jokes I heard when I landed on Earth. You see, I was born on Crouton, a distant planet about the size of Uranus. *The planet* Uranus, that is.

Crouton is much like Earth, with a few exceptions.

For instance, Earth rotates on its axis, while Crouton rotates on a long barbecue skewer like a gigantic rotisserie chicken.

When my rocket ship crash-landed on Earth after the four-day voyage from Crouton, I realized three things:

My dog, Punch, who was in the rocket ship with me, now had the power to speak due to some irregularity in Earth's atmosphere.

My sense of humor, which was always very powerful on Crouton, suddenly had supernatural strength. I had become frighteningly funny.

But most of all, I realized that I had to go to the bathroom really badly.

Punch and I were rescued by a nice man named Bob Foster. Because his name was already Foster, I asked him if he would be my foster father. Bob Foster's response was to suggest that I jump in a lake.

Taking a swim sounded like a terrific idea. I could tell that Bob Foster really cared about my well-being. Later, after Punch and I had dried off, we went over to Bob Foster's house for a visit. Bob Foster invited us to spend the night after we chained ourselves to his coffee table.

The rest, as they say, is history. Bob Foster, Punch, and I have become one big happy family.

I skipped a lot of the details, of course. I didn't tell you anything about the underwear factory. And I didn't tell you about the time Punch peed on Millard Fillmore's rug at the White House. You can read about them in Funny Boy #1 and #2 if you want.

Go ahead. Read those books. The rest of us will wait here. When you finish reading #1 and #2, we'll all move on to the next chapter, and my next adventure.

## CHAPTER 2

# YOU DON'T HAVE TO READ THIS CHAPTER EITHER, BUT YOU MIGHT WANT TO, BECAUSE IT SETS UP THE REST OF THIS RIDICULOUS STORY, AND IF YOU DON'T READ IT, YOU KINDA WON'T KNOW WHAT'S GOING ON LATER.

It all began the day the cows went on strike.

It was a cold and dreary Texas day. The clouds were rolling in on the plains and the wind was blowing furiously.

Not that any of that matters, of course. But books

always seem to say what the weather is like. Don't you just hate that? If you're ever reading a book and the author starts describing the weather, just skip ahead to the next paragraph. Believe me, you won't miss a thing. They just put that stuff in to fill pages.

Anyway, I was telling you about the day the cows went on strike.

It seems that some scientists had used bioengineering to clone a herd of cows that were far more intelligent than normal cows. These cows, it seems, started wondering what we humans were doing with all the milk we were taking away from them every day. When they found that we were not only drinking it but also turning it into cheese, they got really upset. So they

went on strike, refusing to give any more milk until they were given a say on what we humans did with it.

"No pasteurization without representation," they mooed.

Well, to make a long story short, these super-intelligent cows spread the word to the average-intelligent cows. And the average-intelligent cows spread the word to the dumb cows. The dumb cows, not really knowing what to do with this information, told the goats.

The next thing you know, there was a serious worldwide cheese shortage.

What does any of this have to do with aliens attacking Earth? Oh, you're gonna find out. Believe me, you're gonna find out.

The day the cows went on strike, I was making my usual rounds as Funny Boy, walking the streets of San Antonio, Texas, where I live. I was searching for evil-doers so I could rid the world of them.

I was looking pretty sharp in my Funny Boy costume— yellow cape over my pajamas and a fake nose and glasses.

There weren't any evildoers around, which really bummed me out. Without evildoers, there was no need for Funny Boy, just as if there were no car crashes, there would be no need for automotive repair shops.

But suddenly, I spotted a guy who was clearly up to no good.

He was driving an odd-looking little truck slowly down the street. Every so often, he would stop the truck and get out. He had a goofy-looking blue hat on, and a big bag over his shoulder. He got out of the truck and walked up to people's houses. Then, without even asking, he would take some stuff out of his bag and just push it through a slot in the front door. After that, he would just walk away and do the same thing to the next house.

"Halt, evildoer!" I shouted, leaping into his path before he could commit any more crimes.

"What can I do for you, sonny boy?"

"My name is not sonny boy," I informed him. "It's *Funny* Boy. And you're under arrest!"

"What for?"

"Illegal dumping," I snapped. "You can't just throw garbage into people's houses and walk away like nothing happened."

"But I'm a mailman!" the guy protested.

"I'm not falling for that," I retorted with a sneer. "*All men are male men.*"

The guy started laughing, so I knew it would not be long before he had ceased his illegal activities. As you may know, people find it very difficult to commit crimes and laugh at the same time.

"As Funny Boy," I continued, "it is my duty to use jokes and humor to make criminals obey the laws of the land."

"So you're going to tell me jokes?"

"That's right," I replied. "What do you call a boy with three eyes?"

"What?"

"Seymour."

"That's terrible," the man groaned. "Please stop that."

"I have not yet begun to unleash the power of my humor!" I shouted. "Why don't elephants smoke?"

"Why?"

"They can't fit their butts in the ashtray."

"Okay, okay," he whimpered, covering his ears. "I've heard enough. Please stop telling jokes."

"I will stop telling jokes if you stop dumping your trash into other people's houses."

"Anything, anything."

By now you are certainly asking yourself what a cheese shortage and mailmen have to do with aliens attacking Earth. You're probably yelling, "Get to the point!"

Okay, I'll get to the point.

That very night, four enormous cheeses fell from the sky, and one of them landed on top of a mailman in Appleton, Wisconsin.

## CHAPTER 3

# YOU MIGHT WANT TO READ THIS CHAPTER BECAUSE THIS IS WHEN THE ALIENS FIRST ARRIVE AND IT'S REALLY COOL. BUT HEY, IT'S A FREE COUNTRY; AND IF YOU DON'T READ IT, NOBODY'S GONNA PUT YOU IN JAIL OR ANYTHING.

We heard about the falling cheeses because Bob Foster, my dog, Punch, and I were sitting in the living room that night watching the Food Network on TV. They were showing a documentary about eggplant.

"Why do we have to watch the Food Network?"

Punch asked Bob Foster. "You get over a hundred different channels. Can't we watch something else?"

"What's wrong with the Food Network?" Bob asked.

"It's a whole network about *food*!" Punch and I wailed.

"Okay, okay," Bob said, picking up the remote control. "I'll switch to the Weather Channel."

"No!" Punch and I screamed. "Not the Weather Channel!"

At that moment, the words SPECIAL REPORT flashed

on the screen. The three of us stopped arguing. There was a lady on the screen holding a microphone.

"We interrupt 'The History of Eggplant' for this special bulletin," the reporter announced. "This is Pamela Lancashire reporting from Appleton, Wisconsin, where a very strange, unexplainable event has occurred. Let me explain. Minutes ago, four cheeses, each about the size of a school bus, fell from the sky and landed in the parking lot behind this Appleton post office. One of them flattened a mailman named George Gouda."

The camera pulled back to show an enormous wedge of cheese, with a crushed mail truck beneath it.

"Wow!" Punch exclaimed. "In fact, bowwow!"

(Ever since Punch arrived on Earth and realized she could talk, she has refused to bark like normal dogs.)

"Imagine that!" I said. "Cheese falling from the sky!"

"Did I ever tell you that cheese is my hobby?" Bob Foster commented.

"Hobbies are coin collecting and building model cars," I scoffed. "You can't have cheese as a hobby."

"I've always been fascinated by cheese," Bob continued. "Did you know that there are more than two thousand different kinds of cheese?"

"Will you be quiet?" Punch interrupted. "I'm trying to watch TV."

The TV reporter bent down and put her microphone in the face of a mailman who was lying in a huge puddle of cheese. Melted cheese was dripping down his face.

"We have an exclusive interview with the unfortunate letter carrier right now. What happened, Mr. Gouda?"

"*Cheeeeeese*," the man moaned groggily. He looked like he was in shock. "*Cheeeeeeese*."

"Mr. Gouda doesn't appear to be in any condition to talk right now. But we'll have a live interview with him just as soon as he is coherent."

"What does coherent mean?" I asked.

"Something you'll never be," Punch cracked.

---

**NOTE TO READER: Coherent means "speaking or thinking in a way that makes sense." See, you actually learned something! Who says this book has no educational value?**

---

"Back to our studio," the reporter announced, "for the conclusion of 'The History of Eggplant.'"

"Wait!" shouted a voice on TV.

"Who said that?" the reporter asked.

"Me."

"Who's me?"

"I did. The cheese."

The reporter turned around, a puzzled, frightened look on her face. The camera panned down to the cheese. It was a horrifying sight. The cheese didn't have a normal face. At least it didn't have what *we* think of as a normal face. It had five eyes arranged like the Olympic rings. The mouth was a big, gaping hole.

The face was floating around on the cheese. There was no nose.

"A t-talking cheese?" the reporter asked. "A living, breathing cheese?"

"This is the most ridiculous thing I've ever seen," Bob Foster commented.

"How can a cheese talk?"

"This wouldn't be a very interesting book if the cheese didn't talk," Punch quipped.

"Will you two be quiet?" I whispered. "She's going to interview the cheese!"

"Greetings, people of Earth!" The cheese spoke cheerfully, in perfect English. "We come in piece. Ha-ha! Get it? Piece? Peace on Earth? Piece of cheese?"

"That cheese is pretty funny," Bob Foster noted.

"For a cheese," added Punch.

"Do you have a name?" the stunned reporter asked.

"Romano," the cheese replied. "And behind me are my comrades, Mr. Fontina, Mr. Mozzarella, and our leader, Mr. Monterey Jack."

"Y-you are all named after types of cheese?" the reporter asked warily. "Well, what else would we be named after?" Romano asked.

"Where are you from?" the reporter asked.

"Chattanooga."

"Chattanooga, Tennessee?"

"No, the *planet* Chattanooga. It is in another galaxy, forty million light-years from Earth. We have come to rescue your planet."

"Rescue us?" asked the reporter. "From what?"

"The cheese shortage, of course!" replied Fontina.

"Yes," Mozzarella explained. "We understand there is an extreme shortage of cheese on your planet due to some uncooperative cows. We have the ability to clone ourselves and produce unlimited amounts of cheese. We will supply you with all the cheese you need."

"And *that's* why you came to Earth?"

"Well, also because you have cable TV."

"So you're not some evil aliens who want to take over the planet or anything like that?" asked the reporter.

"Ha-ha-ha-ha-ha!" The cheeses all laughed nervously. "Nothing like that at all. We are *friendly* cheeses. Happy cheeses."

"So this is good news for all of us!" bubbled the reporter.

"*Cheeeeeeeeese*," moaned George Gouda.

"Well, good news for *most* of us. Reporting live from Appleton, Wisconsin, this is Pamela Lancashire.

We take you back to 'The History of Eggplant.' It's not an egg. It's not a plant. What is it?"

It was late, and I had to get up for school in the morning. Bob Foster flipped off the TV set, a worried expression on his face.

"I don't know why," Bob Foster whispered, "but something tells me those are *not* normal cheeses."

**[Imagine scary music here.]**

## CHAPTER 4

# IF YOU'RE A BOY, THINK ABOUT SKIPPING THIS CHAPTER, BECAUSE IT'S ABOUT LOVE, LOVE, LOVE! YUCK, DISGUSTING!

It was a beautiful, sun-kissed day, with puffy white clouds hanging in the sky like gigantic cotton candy. But none of that had anything to do with this book, of course.

The news that four alien cheeses had landed in Wisconsin was not a big story at first. When I looked in the newspaper the next morning, the front page headline did not shout in huge letters ALIEN CHEESES

LAND IN WISCONSIN! The headline read SCHOOL BOARD TO HIRE NEW CROSSING GUARDS. In fact, there wasn't even an article anywhere in the paper about an alien landing.

You see, there's something you need to know about the state of Wisconsin. It is the cheese capital of the world.

That's no joke. My foster dad Bob Foster's hobby is cheese, and he knows more about cheese than just about anybody in the world. Bob told me that Wisconsin produces more cheese than any state in America, and more cheese than most entire countries. You've seen those guys at Green Bay Packers football games wearing cheeses on their heads, right? Well, *everybody* in Wisconsin walks around like that.

People reading this book who live in Wisconsin can back me up on this. They produce so much cheese in Wisconsin that they don't know what to do with it all. They eat it for breakfast, lunch, and dinner. They use it as doorstops and paperweights. They stuff it in their mattresses. Kids use it in place of Play-Doh.

In Wisconsin, they don't even use paper money

and coins to buy things. They use cheese. They carry the stuff with them in backpacks wherever they go.

It's true, I say! The word *Wisconsin*, in fact, is an old Indian word that means "land of milk curds."

Just to give you an idea of how important cheese is in Wisconsin, I have prepared the following overview of the state. You may want to clip out this page and use it for your next social studies report:

## STATE PROFILE OF WISCONSIN

*State slogan: America's Dairyland*

*State animal: Cow*

*State food: Duh!*

*State color: Bleu*

*State bird: The Gorgonzola*

*Largest ethnic group: Kurds*

*Most popular TV show: The Muensters*

*Governor: Chuck E. Cheese*

Because they have so much cheese in Wisconsin, it probably wasn't such a big deal when those four giant cheese aliens arrived from outer space. But I live in Texas, and I was sure all the kids would be talking about it at school the next morning.

"It is time for current events," my teacher Mrs. Wonderland announced. "Who has a news story for us today?"

I was the only one who raised a hand.

"Yes, Funny Boy?"

"I don't have a clipping from the newspaper, but last night, four giant cheeses landed on a mailman in Wisconsin."

The class burst out laughing. As I mentioned earlier, something in Earth's atmosphere has made me unbelievably funny. People laugh when I say just about anything because of my super sense of humor.

"I see it's joke time again," Mrs. Wonderland muttered wearily as she rubbed her eyes.

"Joke time?" I said. "Okay, these two guys walk into a bar. You'd think the second one would have ducked."

"Funny Boy," Mrs. Wonderland hissed, "where did you come up with this ridiculous notion that cheeses came from outer space and landed in Wisconsin?"

"I was watching the Food Network—"

Some of the kids in the back of the room interrupted me with laughter.

"What a dork!" said Sal Monella, the biggest and dumbest kid in the class.

"That's enough of that!" Mrs. Wonderland roared, clapping to get everybody's attention. "Let's move on to math. Yesterday we were working on multiplication. Let's review. What is eight times seven?"

I raised my hand and Mrs. Wonderland pointed to me.

"Eight times seven what?" I asked.

"Eight times seven *anything*," Mrs. Wonderland replied. "It's simple. Eight . . . times . . . seven."

"Well, it's not as simple as it seems," I pointed out. "For example, eight times seven pumpkins would be more than eight times seven apples, because pumpkins are bigger than apples. But if you made the apples into applesauce and scooped out the pumpkin seeds, you would probably have more applesauce than pumpkin seeds. See?"

Mrs. Wonderland stared at me for a long time.

"Go to Principal Werner's office," she instructed.

As it turned out, I didn't have to go to Principal Werner's office after all, because Principal Werner saw me coming down the hallway and told me to go jump in a lake. I could tell that physical fitness was very important to Principal Werner, because he was constantly telling me to jump in a lake.

Oddly, there was no lake on the school grounds, so I joined the rest of the class at recess in the playground. A group of the fourth-grade boys were hanging around near the swings, so I joined them.

"I hate girls," Sal Monella told the boys.

"I hate girls, too," one of the others agreed.

"Me, too."

"Me, too."

"Me, too."

"Me, too."

At that moment, this girl walked by. Not just any old girl. This girl was, without a doubt, THE MOST BEAUTIFUL GIRL IN THE WORLD!

Let me try to describe her for you. She had long blond hair, which was curly and dark. She was tall, on the short side. Her body was thin, and just a little overweight. I had never seen anyone like her before.

"I hate girls, too," I agreed. "Who's *that*?"

"It's the new girl. Tupper Camembert," Sal told me. "She just moved in around the corner from me. She's in the other fourth-grade class. This is her first day in school."

"Tupper?" somebody asked. "What kind of a dumb name is Tupper?"

"Who cares? I'm in love!"

"I'm in love!"

"I'm in love!"

"I'm in love!"

"I'm in love!"

"I'm in love!" I proclaimed.

"Forget it," Sal snickered. "Tupper Camembert wouldn't give you the time of day."

"Oh yeah?" I said. "We'll see about that!"

I quickly caught up with Tupper and tapped her on the shoulder.

"Excuse me," I said as charmingly as possible. "Can you please tell me what time it is?"

"No," Tupper replied. "Why don't you go jump in a lake?"

I jogged back over to Sal and the group of boys.

"You were right," I huffed to Sal. "She wouldn't give me the time of day. But she did invite me to go swimming."

"What?" the boys all asked, their mouths open.

"She asked me to jump in a lake," I replied, which for some reason the boys found amusing.

"That means she thinks you're a dork, dork," said Sal.

"Go ahead and laugh," I told them. "1 love Tupper Camembert and none of you will be invited to our eventual wedding. I have seen the girl I will spend the rest of my life with, er, I mean the girl with whom I will spend the rest of my life."

"Huh?"

"Let me shout it from the mountaintops. I'm in love with Tupper Camembert! I will follow her to the ends of the earth. I will follow her until the stars cease to shine. Until the oceans stop waving and the moon stops mooning. I will follow her until Bill Gates runs out of money. Until the Chicago Cubs win the World Series. I love her as no man has ever loved a woman."

"What a dork!" Sal replied as the bell rang.

## CHAPTER 5

# IF YOU'VE READ ALL THE OTHER CHAPTERS, YOU SHOULD BE TOTALLY HOOKED BY NOW AND WILL WANT TO READ THIS ONE, TOO. OR NOT.

It was raining and cold when I got up the next morning. But as you very well know, that had nothing to do with the story. So there was no good reason to bring it up.

The news about the giant alien cheeses wasn't in the papers that day. But it was the *next* day. There was a small item in the food section about these "cute" cheeses that were nice enough to travel 40 million

light-years to provide Earth with all the cheese we'd need until the cheese shortage was over.

I thought that would be the end of it, but the next evening Bob Foster and I were watching the *The Tonight Show,* and who should be on as a guest but Monterey Jack, the leader of the cheeses! They had to build a huge chair for him to "sit" in while Jay Leno interviewed him.

"I must say," Jay Leno said, "Jack, you're the first enormous talking cheese we've had on the show. You certainly are ugly."

"Flattery will get you nowhere, Jay. Beauty is in the eye of the beholder."

"So, do you have a wife or a girlfriend, Jack? What's her name, Velveeta?"

"My lips are sealed."

"I notice you use a lot of clichés when you talk, Jack. You know, tired, overused expressions that have lost their originality and impact because we've heard them so many times."

"I make no bones about it," Jack replied. "If the shoe fits, wear it."

"Don't you ever talk without using clichés?"

"Once in a blue moon."

"When were you born?"

"I wasn't born yesterday, Jay."

"Tell me, what does a cheese eat?"

"You can't have your cake and eat it, too."

"So you're basically a chitchatting, cliché-cracking cheese from Chattanooga."

The audience thought Monterey Jack was a witty and engaging guest. The next week, there was a feature story in *People* magazine about the Wisconsin mailman and the four cheeses that fell on top of him.

*The Guinness Book of World Records* sent a representative to verify that what had fallen out of the Wisconsin sky was in fact the "largest cheese in the world."

On TV, *60 Minutes* devoted a segment to the alien cheeses. They appeared on an episode of *Modern Family*. A parade was held in their honor, and they were hailed as the heroes who had saved America from a real cheese crisis.

It wasn't long before "cheesemania" was sweeping the nation. Sales of all cheese products tripled. Cheese-themed trading cards, T-shirts, and lunch boxes appeared on store shelves. Somebody came out with a rap song about cheese. There was talk of a major motion picture starring Monterey Jack, Romano, Fontina, and Mozzarella. *People* said they could be the hottest thing since Silly Bandz.

Young girls argued about which of the four cheeses was the cutest. Grown women found them to be attractive, too. Monterey Jack received several marriage proposals. There were rumors that he was seen at a nightclub with those tennis-playing Williams sisters.

Everybody, it seemed, loved Monterey Jack, Romano, Fontina, and Mozzarella.

Everybody but my foster father, Bob Foster, the cheese hobbyist and knower of all things about cheese.

"Something tells me," he whispered, shaking his head, "those cheeses are up to no good."

**[Imagine increasingly scary music here.]**

Dorothy Peacock Library
Langley SD35

Dorothy Peacock library
Langley 5D35

# MORE LOVE STUFF HERE. BOYS MIGHT WANT TO SKIP THIS CHAPTER AND MOVE ON TO CHAPTER 7, WHERE THERE'S A LOT OF VIOLENCE AND DESTRUCTION AND DEATH. COOL!

Despite the scary music that ended the last chapter, I didn't concern myself with the enormous cheeses that had landed in Wisconsin and become worldwide celebrities. Monterey Jack, Romano, Fontina, and Mozzarella seemed like happy, harmless cheeses that just happened to have come from outer space. It wasn't like they were evil aliens that were going to take over Earth or anything. Nothing to worry my little head about.

Besides, I had something else on my mind. Tupper Camembert.

I was in love! I let the sound of her name roll around in my mouth. Tup-per Cam-em-bert. Tup-per Cam-em-bert. Say it loud and there's music playing! Say it soft and it's almost like praying.

I had never had this feeling in my life. Tupper was so beautiful! I couldn't get the picture of her out of my mind. I thought about her day and night. I couldn't concentrate on anything else. I dreamed about her.

Tup-per Cam-em-bert. Tup-per Cam-em-bert.

"Will you stop it?" my dog, Punch, snapped as I was writing Tupper's name over and over again on my hand with indelible marker. "That stupid name is giving me a headache."

"How dare you call the girl I love stupid!"

"It's *you* who's stupid!" Punch barked.

I tackled Punch, and she began biting me on the leg. We rolled around on the floor for a few minutes before Bob Foster came in to see what all the fuss was about.

"I think we should have a little talk," Bob Foster told me after he had broken up the fight. Punch stormed out of my room in a huff.

Bob Foster sat on my bed with me. "It's time you learned about the birds and the bees."

"I'm not interested in animals," I replied. "I want to know about girls."

"No, what I mean is, it's time I told you the facts of life."

"Huh?"

"You see, Funny Boy, the purpose of a man is to love a woman. You follow me?"

"Uh-huh."

"And the purpose of a woman is to love a man."

"Okay . . ."

I didn't quite catch the rest, because Bob got up and started singing and dancing around my bedroom like a lunatic.

Eventually, Bob Foster regained control of himself and sat back down on the bed.

"I love Tupper Camembert," I complained. "But she won't give me the time of day."

"Look," Bob Foster said, putting his arm around

my shoulder. "You're still new to this planet. You gotta understand the way the game of love works. If this girl is acting like she's not interested in you, that means just one thing—she is totally in love with you. Don't you see it? She's just playing hard to get."

"Hard to get? What does that mean?"

"When a girl likes a boy, she pretends she can't stand him. And when a boy likes a girl, he pretends he can't stand her. That's the way the game works. So if this girl acts like she can't stand you, that is a sign that she is in love with you."

"Either that," Punch shouted from the next room, "or she just can't stand you."

"But it doesn't make any sense," I told Bob Foster. "If somebody really likes somebody else, why don't they just come out and say so?"

"That's the game of love." Bob Foster grinned, shaking his head and chuckling. "Girls want to be chased. She wants you to pursue her."

I decided to put Bob Foster's theory to the test. When school let out the next day, I spotted Tupper Camembert walking home. I didn't follow her, because I didn't want her to know I was trying to catch up with her. Instead, I ran around the block so she would have to bump into me and it would look like she was following me.

"Hi, Tupper," I declared. "Are you following me home?"

"No."

I thought that if I told a joke, it might loosen Tupper up a little.

"What did one plate say to the other?" I asked.

"What?"

"Lunch is on me."

She wrinkled up her nose, as if she had smelled something really bad.

That's good, I said to myself. The fact that she hadn't laughed at the joke meant she really liked it. Maybe Bob Foster was right. Now I had to show Tupper that I didn't have the least interest in her.

"You don't want to go out for dinner with me sometime, do you?" I asked.

"No, I don't."

"Don't give me your answer right now," I interrupted. "Take your time and think it over."

"I did. The answer is no."

"Good," I replied. "I don't want to have dinner with you either. I just wanted to make sure we were in agreement. You don't want to go out for lunch, do you?"

"No."

"What a coincidence. Me neither," I replied. "What about breakfast?"

"No."

"Great!" I exclaimed. "You know, Tupper, I think you and I have really hit it off. We have a lot in common. You don't want to go out with me, and I don't want to go out with you either. We're the perfect couple."

Tupper just stared at me like I was from another planet, which made sense because I *was* from another planet.

"What about a snack?" I asked. "You wouldn't be interested in joining me for an after-school snack, would you?"

"No," she replied. "Will you leave me alone, please?"

"You don't eat much, do you, Tupper?"

"Look, why don't you take a long walk off a short pier?"

Boy, Earthlings certainly do enjoy water sports! I couldn't get over it. Back home on Crouton, we used to swim once in a while when the weather was hot. But here on Earth, people must go swimming all the time. I was constantly being told to jump into lakes, dive off cliffs, soak my head, and take long walks off short piers.

I remembered what Bob Foster had told me. Tupper was playing hard to get. Deep down inside she felt the same way about me as I felt about her.

This was great. She was acting like she really couldn't stand me. So she must truly be in love with me. Things were going perfectly according to plan! If I just kept it up, eventually Tupper would admit her love for me and we would live happily ever after. That is, unless something really horrible happened to mess everything up.

And then something really horrible happened to mess everything up.

## CHAPTER 7

# IF YOU'RE A GIRL THINK ABOUT SKIPPING THIS CHAPTER, UNLESS YOU'RE THE KIND OF GIRL WHO HATES THE LOVE STUFF AND LIKES VIOLENCE AND DESTRUCTION AND DEATH.

Around seven o'clock the next evening, in the town of Cape May at the southernmost tip of New Jersey, precipitation began to fall from the sky.

Now, you may think the weather had nothing to do with this story. In fact, it had *everything* to do with this story.

Ordinarily, the word "precipitation" means rain or snow. But what fell from the sky were little flecks of cheddar cheese.

At first, nobody noticed anything unusual. It looked like snow flurries. But gradually, people realized it wasn't snow at all.

A little girl stuck out her tongue to catch a snow-flake, and she spat it out immediately. A driver flipped on his windshield wiper and found that it smeared the flakes across the windshield. A lady felt some flakes land on her arms and wondered why they didn't feel cold.

The cheese stuck to the ground and soon the town of Cape May was blanketed in white. Friends started calling other friends on the phone, and people came running out of their houses to see if the raining cheese was some kind of joke. In minutes, the whole town knew the truth.

New Jersey was getting cheesed.

The cheese storm moved up the coastline and soon accumulations of three inches of cheese were reported all over the state. Trenton, the state capital, was cheesed in. Northern New Jersey was paralyzed.

At first people thought it was funny. Kids cele-brated because they wouldn't have to go to school the next day. They had cheese-ball fights and built cheese-men in their backyards. Some people started shoveling the cheese off their driveways or brushing it off their cars so they would be able to drive to work in the morning.

But there would be no work the next morning. By six o'clock, the National Weather Service reported that a foot of cheese had fallen on some parts of New Jersey, with drifts as high as three feet. All the schools in the state were closed.

It didn't stop. It got worse. Big globs of cheddar cheese fell from the sky. Cars got stuck in it. It clogged up sewers and chimneys. People couldn't open up their front doors to get outside. The brave souls who tried to trudge through all the cheese to get to super-markets found their boots got stuck in the glop until they couldn't move. It wouldn't have mattered anyway, as all the supermarkets were shut down and boarded up to prevent looting.

The Garden State Parkway, a highway that crosses the state from top to bottom, became a river of cheese.

Cars just stopped in the middle of the road with cheese up to the axles. Tow trucks couldn't move.

Newark Airport was closed. The Lincoln and Holland tunnels going into New York City were closed. So was the George Washington Bridge. Bus and train service was halted. Police, fire, and ambulance crews prepared for the worst.

As temperatures got higher during the day, the cheese began to melt slightly. By noon it was a sloppy, oozing, gooey mess. Helicopters flying overhead reported that the state of New Jersey looked like a giant undercooked pizza.

The most amazing thing was, New Jersey was the only state that got cheesed. Not a drop fell on Pennsylvania, New York, or Delaware, all of which border the state.

The rest of the country watched what was happening with amazement and horror. JERSEY GETS CHEESED! shouted the headline of the *New York Post*. Emergency crews rushed to the state to rescue people who were trapped inside their houses. When the President declared the entire state of New Jersey to be a disaster area, comedians joked that they'd thought New Jersey already *was* a disaster area.

I watched the cheese storm on the Weather Channel with Bob Foster and my dog, Punch.

"What could be causing it?" Punch asked. "Cheese doesn't just fall from the sky."

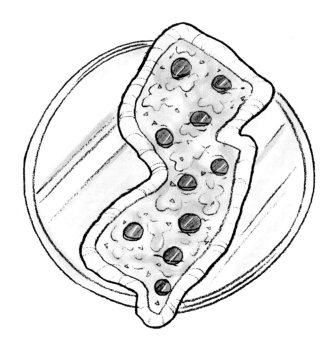

"Maybe it's a hoax," I guessed.

"It's no hoax," Bob Foster replied, with a worried expression on his face. "It has something to do with those cheeses in Wisconsin. I told you they weren't just normal cheeses."

---

**Cheesy trivia from Bob Foster: 80 percent of the cheese made in the United States is cheddar. Cheddar cheese is named for a village in southwestern England, where they have made this kind of cheese since the 12th century!**

---

## CHAPTER 8

# IF YOU MAKE IT TO THE END OF THIS CHAPTER, YOU'LL BE HALFWAY THROUGH THIS STUPID BOOK. THAT'S NOTHING TO BRAG ABOUT, MIND YOU.

The cheese storm that devastated New Jersey stunned and shocked the nation. We watched the horrifying images on TV that evening.

Hundred-year-old trees had been toppled over by tons of melted cheese clinging to their branches. Houses were almost completely covered by enormous mounds of cheese. We saw people standing on their rooftops waving to be rescued. It was very upsetting, especially to Bob Foster, whose hobby was cheese.

It seemed fairly obvious that Monterey Jack, Romano, Fontina, and Mozzarella had something to do with what had happened in New Jersey. The alien cheeses, we realized now, had *not* come to Earth to help America through our cheese shortage. Oh no, that was just a story they made up to mask their true intentions.

We had to face reality. Monterey Jack, Romano, Fontina, and Mozzarella were evil. And they were angry. They clearly had other plans for Earth. We just didn't know what those plans were yet.

It was quiet around the dinner table that evening. Bob Foster, who liked to serve cheese at just about every meal, prepared a cheese-free dinner. We discussed how lucky we were to be living in Texas, so far away from the gooey cheese fields of New Jersey. Even I wasn't in the mood to crack any jokes.

"Let me think," Bob Foster said, rubbing his chin. "Cheese is very high in protein and rich in calcium and vitamin A. . . ."

"So?" Punch asked.

"What does that have to do with what happened?"

"I'm just trying to figure out what we can do to stop this insane cheese menace."

"They're alien cheeses, right?" Punch asked. "Well, there's only one person who can stop aliens."

I was just about to eat a spoonful of my Spaghet-tiOs when I realized that Bob Foster and Punch were staring at me.

"Funny Boy," Punch urged, "you've got to do something!"

"Me? Wh-what can I do?"

"You defeated the airsick alien, didn't you?" Punch asked.

"Yeah, she was no match for my sense of humor."

"You defeated those bubble-brained barbers, didn't you?" Bob Foster asked.

"I just told them jokes," I explained. "What do you expect me to do, tell jokes to a *cheese*?"

"Yes!" Punch and Bob Foster shouted at the same time.

I didn't think it would work. Reluctantly, I agreed to use the superpower of my sense of humor to battle the cheeses.

But first we had to find them. When the dinner dishes had been cleared away, Bob Foster tuned his TV in to

CNN. The cheesing of New Jersey was the top story, but CNN reported that the cheeses had gone into hiding.

It was the same on ABC, CBS, NBC, TNT, HBO, PBS, and every other network with three initials. None of them had been able to locate the cheeses for an interview. Suddenly, the cheeses weren't talking.

When the news was over, Bob Foster flipped to the Food Channel for a few minutes before bedtime. They were in the middle of a cooking show with Chef Rick Cotta when suddenly the picture went blank. A moment passed, and then Mozzarella's ugly "face" filled the screen.

"Listen here, Earthlings! Now our true story can be told. You have angered us! No more Mr. Nice Cheese. Now we are going to make you pay."

Chef Cotta was now tied to a chair and covered with a giant glop of cheese.

"B-but why are you so angry?" Chef Cotta asked through the cheese that was dripping down his face. "What have we done to you?"

"You *eat* cheese!" Mozzarella thundered.

"I beg your pardon?"

"You eat cheese!" Mozzarella repeated. "And we *are* cheese!"

"You mean you are angry because we eat your kind?" the chef asked, disbelieving.

"He's pretty smart, for a human," snickered Fontina.

"W-we never realized that cheese had feelings," the chef admitted.

"How do you think we feel when you grill us, fry us, grate us, melt us, and dribble us on tortilla chips to make nachos?" asked Mozzarella. "It's disgusting!"

"How would you like it if you came to *our* planet

and found we ate human beings?" asked Fontina. "What if we ate grilled human sandwiches? What if we made macaroni-and-human dinners for our children? How would you feel if we spread humans on bagels, put you on crackers, and cooked you on pizzas? What if we munched on Human Doodles?"

"B-b-but . . . there are hundreds of different kinds of cheeses," Chef Cotta asked. "There must be at least one that you will allow us to eat."

"There is only one kind of cheese that we despise . . . American cheese! And now America and the planet Earth must die!"

"B-b-but . . . w-we had no idea."

"It is too late for apologies, Earthling! The cheesing of New Jersey was just a small demonstration of our power. If you do not give us what we want, we will unleash the full fury of our cheese arsenal and you will be extremely sorry you crossed us."

"What do you want? What are your demands?"

"I'm not going to negotiate with a chef even if you do have your own TV show. Bring us . . . the President of the United States of America!"

Congratulations! It's halftime. You have reached the exact middle point of this book. This would be a good time to stretch your legs, have a snack, use the bathroom, and so on. Enjoy the second half!

## CHAPTER 9

# I'M GETTING TIRED OF THINKING UP THESE DUMB CHAPTER TITLES. JUST KEEP READING AND LEAVE ME ALONE, OKAY?

Five minutes after the alien cheeses demanded on national TV to speak to the President of the United States, the phone rang in Bob Foster's kitchen. Bob Foster picked it up.

"It's President Purgallin!" Bob Foster whispered, handing me the phone excitedly.

"Funny Boy, this is Myles Purgallin," the President barked.

"Yes, sir!" I blurted, snapping to attention.

"I need you to meet me in Appleton, Wisconsin, first thing in the morning!"

Wow! A national emergency takes place and the first person the President of the United States calls is *me*. What an honor. It was the most exciting moment of my life. My heart was pounding.

"I've got school in the morning," I told President Purgallin. "How about Saturday?"

"Earth may be destroyed by Saturday!"

This is great, I thought to myself! If Earth were destroyed by Saturday, I wouldn't ever have to do homework again! I wouldn't have to deal with teachers or books or pencils or report cards because we'd all be dead and . . .

"I'll be right there," I told the President.

Quickly, Bob Foster wrote a note to my teacher:

DEAR MRS. WONDERLAND,

PLEASE EXCUSE FUNNY BOY FROM SCHOOL

TODAY. HE HAS TO GO TO WISCONSIN TO

PREVENT GIANT CHEESES FROM TAKING

OVER EARTH. I WILL PICK UP HIS HOMEWORK

TOMORROW, UNLESS OF COURSE THE WORLD

IS DESTROYED LATER THIS AFTERNOON.

SINCERELY,

BOB FOSTER

Bob Foster, Punch, and I rushed to Wisconsin for our meeting with President Purgallin.

"Did you know," Bob Foster informed us as we boarded the plane, "that the average American eats ten pounds of cheese each year?"

"Will you knock it off?" Punch screeched. "The whole planet is gonna be destroyed, and you're giving us cheese trivia."

A long white limousine was waiting for us when we got off the plane. A Secret Service agent hopped out and opened the door for us. The President was waiting inside the car.

"Good to see you again, Funny Kid," the President said, sticking out his hand.

"That's Funny Boy, sir," I corrected him.

"Whatever. As you know, Earth is being threatened by some enormous cheeses from outer space. Once again I need your unique gift of humor to repel this threat to our existence."

"I'll do my best, sir."

"Mr. President," Bob Foster commented, "speaking of cheese, did you know that in the country of Tibet, yaks supply milk for cheese? Cheese is also made from donkey milk, zebra milk, and camel milk."

The President looked at Bob Foster for a long moment.

"Who is this guy?" he asked.

"That's Bob Foster, sir. Remember? He's my foster father. He knows a lot about cheese. Maybe he can help us defeat this cheese menace."

"You've got to know what you're up against, Mr. President," Bob Foster said. "Who was it who once said, 'Know thy enemy'?"

"Somebody with bad grammar," the President grunted.

The President looked like he was in a bad mood. It must be difficult running the country, it occurred to me. Every day you have to deal with the economy, Congress, conflicts with other nations, domestic problems. He certainly had enough problems to deal with. And now, enormous cheeses.

The limo pulled onto the highway, WELCOME TO WISCONSIN, a billboard read, AMERICA'S DAIRYLAND.

"I hate cheese," the President muttered.

It wasn't long before we had reached Appleton. The limo pulled up to a large barn, which the cheeses were apparently using as their headquarters for world domination.

"Let me do the talking," the President told me. "I'll find out what they're up to. Then we'll have you use your super power of humor."

"Okay."

The barn door opened and we walked inside. And there they were. Four enormous cheeses, dripping and oozing. They looked even bigger than they did on TV. And they were certainly smellier. The odor was overpowering. It was disgusting. I used my cape to cover my nose.

"So this is the President of the United States," Romano snickered, sliding toward us.

"The most powerful man in the world," drawled Mozzarella.

"Is he the best Earth can offer?" Fontina snorted.

"Beggars can't be choosers," snickered Monterey Jack.

"He's got some friends with him, I see," added Mozzarella.

"I don't have time for small talk," the President snapped. "Which one of you is the big cheese?"

"I am," all four cheeses replied.

The President boldly walked up to the cheeses.

"I understand you are upset because we Earthlings eat cheese," he stated. "Do you plan to take away all our cheese to prevent us from eating you again?"

"Hahahahahahahahahahahahahaha!" the cheeses chortled.

"Just the opposite, Mr. President." Fontina grinned gleefully. "Just the opposite!"

"Tell 'em the plan," Mozzarella smirked.

"Yesterday, we covered your state of New Jersey with a thick layer of cheddar," Romano reminded us.

"Next we will do the same to the rest of the United States. Then we will cover your entire planet, until Earth is one gigantic—cheese ball!"

"That's horrible!" Bob Foster groaned.

"All's fair in love and war," commented Monterey Jack.

"It's gonna be Earth parmigiana!" Mozzarella cracked.

"Hahahahahahahahahahahahaha!" the other cheeses laughed.

"When Earth is entirely covered by cheese," Romano continued, "it will block off the rays of the sun. This will trigger massive global cooling. The temperature of your planet will drop lower and lower. It will be another Ice Age! Earth will become uninhabitable and all human life will cease to exist!"

"Welcome to the Cheese Millennium!" Mozzarella cracked.

"Hahahahahahahahahahahahaha!" the other cheeses laughed.

"Good plan, eh?" asked Mozzarella.

"That's the stupidest plan I ever heard in my life," I told him honestly.

"Who asked you, fake-nose boy?"

"These cheeses are nuts," Bob whispered to me.

"You'd better have some good jokes this time, or we're finished."

"What are your demands?" the President asked grimly.

"Our demands are simple," Fontina replied. "One, you must stop the manufacture, distribution, and sale of all cheese. Two, you must make the eating of cheese punishable by death. Three, you must turn the Smithsonian Institution into the National Museum of Cheese. And four, you must change the Pledge of Allegiance to read as follows: I pledge allegiance to the cheese, who rules the United States of America, and to the Fondue for which it stands, one Nation, individually wrapped, with curds and whey for all."

"That's ridiculous!" the President snapped. "It's out of the question."

"So you refuse to give in to our demands?"

"I have listened to your silly demands," the President warned. "Now you must listen to *this*."

The President gave me a shove forward. I was now face-to-face with the largest cheese in the world.

"Uh, yes," I stammered. "My name is Funny Boy. And I will defeat you by using my advanced sense of humor."

"Your *what?*"

"Jokes, puns, quips, wisecracks," the President answered. "After Funny Boy gets you laughing, you will see the folly of your ways and leave the good people of Earth alone."

"You must be joking," Romano replied.

"Of course I'm joking!" I agreed. "That's why they call me Funny Boy."

"Go ahead," the President urged. "Tell him one of those jokes of yours."

I happened to have just finished reading a book titled *Milton Berle's Private Joke File,* which was filled with over ten thousand jokes for every occasion. I tried to recall a few of the better ones.

"A father told his son that if he behaved, he could grow up to be just like Lincoln. The kid replied, 'Who wants to be a tunnel?'"

The cheeses just stared at me.

"It's not working!" the President whispered to me. "Try another one."

"I know a kid who was so dumb," I quipped, "he didn't know he was ten until he was twelve."

Nothing. Zip. Zero. Not even a smile.

"You know," I continued, "when I was little I was so

skinny that I had to stand next to my brother to have a shadow."

"Your jokes are tiresome!" Mozzarella thundered. "Let the cheesing of America begin!"

I glanced out the barn door. White flakes had started to fall from the sky.

"Let's get out of here!" the President shouted. "Run for your lives!"

"Cheese it!" yelled Bob Foster.

**Cheesy trivia from Bob Foster: The first cheese factory in the United States was started by a man named Jesse Williams in Rome, New York, in 1851!**

## CHAPTER 10

# THINGS START GETTING REALLY SILLY HERE, AND WILL ONLY GET SILLIER. IF YOU HAVE ANY SENSE, YOU'LL TURN BACK AND GRAB ONE OF THOSE NEWBERY BOOKS THAT GROWN-UPS THINK YOU SHOULD BE READING INSTEAD OF THIS JUNK.

By the time we got to the airport in Appleton, flakes of falling cheese were starting to stick to the ground. The wheels of the limousine were beginning to skid around the corners, and the driver was struggling to see through the cheese-smeared windshield.

Air Force One, the President's private plane, was

waiting on the runway when we arrived. We ran to it, slipping on the cheese-covered tarmac with every step.

The air traffic controllers didn't want to let the plane take off, but the President declared the situation a national emergency and forced them to let us go. Slipping and skidding on the cheesy runway, the plane barely made it off the ground.

I took a seat next to the President. He was looking out the window thoughtfully, watching the flakes of cheese blanket the state of Wisconsin.

"I failed you, Mr. President," I admitted sadly.

The President turned to me, with sympathy and understanding in his eyes. He put his hand gently on my shoulder.

"You're right," he said. "You screwed up everything. You're a loser and a dope. Worse than that, you're not the least bit funny. I can't believe I entrusted the fate of the nation to a dumb kid with a yellow cape and a fake nose and glasses. What could I have been thinking? Now leave me alone before I start to choke you."

Almost in tears, I left the President's side and moved to the rear of the plane, where Punch and Bob Foster were gazing out their window.

"I was just thinking," Punch was telling Bob.

"About what?" Bob replied.

"Two things. First, I was thinking about invisible ink. If it's invisible, how do you know when you've run out of it? Second, I was thinking about how many perfectly good trees they had to cut down to print this stupid book. And how many electrons must be wasted for the e-book version?"

"How can you be worrying about things like that at a time like this?" I complained. "The world is about to end! And it's all my fault."

"Don't feel bad," Bob Foster consoled me. "You gave it your best shot."

"Yeah," agreed Punch. "It's not your fault that those jokes were so terrible. Blame it on Milton Berle."

Air Force One has a big-screen television set, and the pilot must have turned it on. Bob Foster's favorite channel—the Weather Channel—was on. A lady was standing in front of a map of the United States. Instead of clouds floating over the country, there were a bunch of cheese wedges.

". . . a forty percent chance of cheese across the Midwest tonight," she announced, "with accumulations of twelve inches or more in Wisconsin, Minnesota, and Iowa. You can expect the cheese storm to taper off after midnight, and then the cheese should start falling across the Northeast and Gulf Coast states. So take along an umbrella, and a cheese grater in case you need to dig out your car. Roads are expected to be slippery, and extremely smelly. Stay tuned for the five-day forecast, in the unlikely event that our planet lasts that long. . . ."

I was too depressed to watch the rest of the weather report. I had failed my President, and I had failed my adopted planet. I wasn't feeling funny at all. It was only a matter of time before Earth would be completely covered in cheese. And there was nothing I could do about it.

There was a phone built in to the seat in front of me. I picked it up. A White House operator came on and asked me who I wanted to speak with. I gave her the name of the one person I cared about most in this time of need. The love of my life—Tupper Camembert.

"How did you get my number?" Tupper asked when I told her who I was.

"Never mind that," I snapped. "Is anything falling from the sky in Texas yet?"

"No, why?"

"Tupper, I'm flying over Wisconsin, and it's getting cheesed just like New Jersey did yesterday. Soon the whole country and the whole world will be one big cheese ball."

"Very funny."

"This is serious, Tupper. I'm in Air Force One right now. I was just chatting with the President."

"If you think that's going to impress me, you're wrong," Tupper hissed. "Don't you get it? I don't want to be your girlfriend. I wouldn't be your girlfriend if the world were going to end tomorrow."

"But, Tupper," I pleaded, "that's why I'm calling. There's a good possibility the world *is* going to end tomorrow. Before that happens, I just wanted to tell you how much I love you."

*Click.* She hung up on me.

---

**Cheesy trivia from Bob Foster: The first cheese was probably made more than four thousand years ago by nomadic tribes in Asia!**

---

**CHAPTER 11**

# THIS CHAPTER IS TOTALLY RIDICULOUS. CLEARLY IT IS THE PRODUCT OF A SICK MIND.

The cheese hadn't started falling in Washington yet when we touched down at Ronald Reagan Airport. A limo whisked us all to the White House, where the President had called an emergency press conference to brief the nation on what was happening.

Bob Foster, Punch, and I gathered in the East Room of the White House. Hundreds of reporters and photographers were already there, anxiously awaiting the President's opening words.

"My fellow Americans," he said somberly, "I come before you with a heavy heart. We are in a time of national emergency.

"A few short days ago some rather large, malodorous cheeses fell out of the sky and landed behind a post office in Wisconsin. Nobody thought much of it at the time. However, since then we have learned that these cheeses are living, breathing creatures from another planet. And they are angry.

"The covering of New Jersey and Wisconsin with cheese over the last few days was only the beginning. My fellow Americans, these cheeses intend to coat our entire world with cheese, block out the sun, and set off a new Ice Age that will wipe out all life on planet Earth."

A gasp was heard from the reporters and photographers. Hands shot in the air to ask questions, but the President gestured for the reporters to let him finish his statement.

"I just wanted to let all of America know that our government does not negotiate with terrorists. We are not going to stand idly by and let some *cheese* push us around. We will not allow ourselves to be intimidated by a snack food. If we could defeat the Nazis in World War II, we can defeat *cheese*. If we could put a man on the moon, we can defeat *cheese*. If we could cure the common cold, we can defeat *cheese*. . . ."

"Mr. President," a reporter chimed. "We haven't cured the common cold yet, sir."

"I knew that," the President affirmed. "I just wanted to see if you were paying attention. The point is, we will defeat this cheese, if we have to destroy the entire planet to do it. I will take a few questions now. But let me say this. If any of these questions get silly, I'll end the press conference right there."

In the back row next to me, my dog, Punch, immediately raised her paw. I held it down, and the President called on one of the reporters instead.

"Mr. President, how do you intend to battle this enemy?"

"That's top secret at this time. I will disclose that information tomorrow morning, first thing."

"What are the aliens' demands, Mr. President?"

"They demand that we stop eating cheese, we build a museum to cheese, and we change the pledge of allegiance to honor them instead of our flag. But as I have said, the United States does not negotiate with terrorists."

"What kind of cheese are they, sir?"

"Apparently there are four kinds. Monterey Jack, Romano, Fontina, and Mozzarella."

Punch tried raising her paw again, but I held it down.

"Mr. President, is this the biggest threat to our civilization since that guy who sang 'Mambo Number Five'?"

"I'm not quite sure what that means," the President replied. "But it sounds like it might be a silly question."

"If the world comes to an end, sir, will it help or hurt your approval rating?"

"That sounds awfully silly!" the President warned. "You know, I could clear this room in a minute."

Punch raised her paw before I could hold it down, and the President called on her.

"If the world does come to an end, will the Funny Boy series continue?"

"Punch!" I whispered.

"I beg your pardon?" asked the President.

"The book you're in. It's part of a series for kids," said Punch.

"Book? Series? I don't know what you're talking about."

"You're a fictional character, Mr. President. In fact, we all are."

"That's it. I've had enough of this. No more press conferences. Somebody get that dog out of here!"

When the press conference broke up, I told Punch and Bob Foster that we should go back to Texas. There was nothing we could do to help in Washington. If Earth was going to be destroyed, we might as well watch the devastation from our adopted home. Besides, I wanted to see the love of my life, Tupper Camembert, one more time before the end of civilization.

"Nothing doing," one of the President's assistants said when Bob Foster asked about a ride to the airport. "The President says he wants you right here in the White House where he can keep an eye on you."

The next morning, as soon as the sun came up, Bob Foster, Punch, and I were escorted into the War Room at the White House. There was a big map of the United States in there. It indicated which parts of the country were already covered with cheese and which parts weren't. Television monitors were positioned around the country so the President could see what was happening everywhere.

At precisely nine o'clock, Operation Cheese Shield began.

Hundreds of Navy helicopters arrived in Wisconsin. They were carrying an enormous box of Saran Wrap. It was nearly a mile wide. Carefully, the end of the Saran Wrap was pulled from the box by four helicopters and unrolled. When several miles of the clear wrap had been stretched across the sky, the helicopters lowered it slowly to the cheese-covered ground. It was apparent that they hoped to contain the cheese by wrapping it up in plastic and then disposing of it in some way.

"It's working!" one of the generals in the War Room shouted. "It's going to work!"

But just before the helicopters touched down, one of the corners of the Saran Wrap came loose. It flopped around in the air currents caused by the propeller blades. Then it flew up and stuck to the middle of the Saran Wrap.

"It's clinging to itself!" the President yelled disgustedly. "I hate it when that happens!"

Soon the rest of the Saran Wrap came loose and the whole thing crumpled together. It was impossible to untangle it. The Navy helicopters dropped the useless wrap to the ground harmlessly. A groan of frustration was heard throughout the War Room.

Next, the Air Force flew in two of the biggest slices of white bread I had ever seen. Each slice was about the size of a football field.

"What are they going to do with those?" I asked Bob Foster.

"It looks like they're trying to surround the cheese with bread and make an enormous cheese sandwich," he replied.

That's exactly what they were doing. It seemed to be working, too. When the two pieces of bread were in place around the cheese, soldiers carrying flamethrowers shot fire at it.

"They're grilling the cheese!" Punch exclaimed excitedly. "They're making a gigantic grilled-cheese sandwich!"

Suddenly, the fire from one of the flamethrowers caught on a corner of the bread. It burned quickly, turning black and spitting smoke everywhere. Soon the whole slice of bread was burned and began breaking into pieces. The sandwich was a big, oozing, smoking, stinky mess.

Next, the Marines brought some huge Saltine crackers strapped to the roof of a tank, but they crumbled when the cheese was shoved on top of them with a bulldozer.

The mood in the War Room was grim. The cheese was still spreading, and there was no way to contain it. Operation Cheese Shield had failed.

"Wait!" the President thundered, snapping his fingers excitedly. "I've got an idea!"

The generals gathered around the President, and within minutes, Operation Cheese Storm had begun. Helicopters flew in carrying enormous vats of pickles, lettuce, ketchup, onions, ground beef, and special sauce. They dropped tons and tons of the stuff right on top of the cheese.

"What are they doing that for?" Punch asked.

"I think their plan," Bob Foster explained, "is to dump so much stuff together that you barely notice how terrible it all is."

"You mean, like a burger in a fast-food restaurant?"

"Exactly!"

Unfortunately, it didn't work. The pickles, ketchup, and other condiments just settled into the cheese and disappeared.

"Quick! Release the macaroni!" one of the generals shouted. "It's our only hope!"

"Macaroni?" I asked. "Didn't he invent the wireless?"

"That was Marconi, you idiot!" Punch told me.

The macaroni-and-cheese plan, whatever it was, didn't work either. The cheese just kept spreading wider and wider. Gloom fell over the War Room.

"It's just some lousy *cheese*!" the President exclaimed, pacing the room. "There must be some way we can contain it."

"Maybe we could breed some gigantic mice," one of the President's advisers suggested. "And they could *eat* the cheese."

"That would take months," the President replied. "Maybe years. We're running out of time. Earth will be completely covered by cheese in a matter of days."

"What are we going to do, sir?" somebody asked.

"I don't know," the President moaned. "I just don't know."

---

**Cheesy trivia from Bob Foster: The holes in Swiss cheese are created by bacteria that are added to the cheese and produce bubbles of carbon dioxide!**

## CHAPTER 12

---

# IF YOU MADE IT THIS FAR, YOU ARE TRULY A GLUTTON FOR PUNISHMENT. YOU SHOULD GET AN AWARD OR SOMETHING.

It was a long day. Everything the military had done in their effort to contain the cheese had failed. It kept covering more and more of the country. By the end of the day, the midwestern United States was almost completely covered with cheese. Cheese storms had begun in California and Florida.

I had the White House operator get Tupper Camembert on the phone again. I wanted to speak with her one last time before the telephone lines in Texas were knocked out by tons and tons of cheese.

"Tupper, it's me, Funny Boy."

"What do you want?"

"I'm at the White House. I just wanted to see if I could comfort you in this time of need. Is there anything I can do to make these last few days on Earth pleasant ones for you?"

"Yes," Tupper told me. "Drop dead, dork."

I hung up the phone and sat down heavily. There are times in a person's life when one has to admit a mistake. Bob Foster's theory about men and women, I finally realized, was all wrong. People are basically honest. When Tupper Camembert had told me to leave her alone and go jump in a lake, it wasn't her way of telling me how much she loved me. It was her way of telling me to leave her alone and go jump in a lake. Tupper Camembert had *never* liked me. I had been a fool.

I had never been so depressed in my life. The world was coming to an end, and I didn't have anyone to share it with.

Sadly, I trudged into the East Room of the White House, where the President was preparing to hold

another press conference. He didn't look so good himself. I took a seat in the back, away from Bob Foster.
Away from Punch. Away from everybody. I just wanted
to be alone.

"My fellow Americans," the President began. "By
now, some of our great United States are completely
submerged under a thick layer of pungent cheese.
The rest of the country, and the world, will soon be
in the same situation. My advisers and I have been up
all night discussing what we should do. At this point,
our only option left is to use nuclear weapons against
the cheese. But I can't do that. It would mean drop-
ping bombs on the United States itself which would
kill every man, woman, and child. So this is what I have
decided to do. . . ."

The President took a deep breath and wiped a tear
from his eye before continuing.

"Effective immediately, the manufacture, distribution, and sale of all cheese is prohibited."

A gasp was heard throughout the room.

"The eating of cheese is punishable by death. The
Smithsonian Institution will be turned into the National
Museum of Cheese. At this point, I would like everyone
to please rise and put your right hand over your heart."

Everybody stood up.

"I pledge allegiance," he recited, "to the cheese—"

"Wait!"

All heads turned around to see who had interrupted the President.

It was my dog, Punch.

"You can't give in yet, Mr. President!" Punch yelped. "We still have one secret weapon at our disposal."

"Who said that?" the President asked, peering into all the faces.

"My name is Punch," Punch yelped. "I'm just

a concerned talking dog who loves her adopted planet."

"And what secret weapon do you have in mind?"

"Funny Boy, sir!" Punch shouted excitedly. "He can beat those cheeses. I just know he can!"

Everyone in the room turned around and stared at me. I gave a little embarrassed wave.

"Funny Boy?" The President snorted. "He failed miserably the last time I gave him a chance. What makes you think he can defeat the cheeses now?"

"I'll tell you why, sir," Punch explained, standing up on her hind legs. "There are only twenty pages left in this book, so Funny Boy *has* to defeat the aliens, and quickly!"

"What book?" the President shouted.

"The book we're all in," explained Punch. "Remember I told you we are all fictional characters?"

The President conferred with his top advisers, who apparently confirmed for him that they were all fictional characters in a children's book.

"How many pages did you say are left in the book?" the President asked.

"Still twenty, sir," Punch echoed.

"Funny Boy, come here!" the President ordered.

All eyes were on me as I walked slowly up the aisle

and climbed up to the podium. I felt so nervous that I was shaking.

"Funny Boy," the President sighed. "I want to apologize for calling you a loser and a dope."

"Apology accepted, Mr. President," I replied.

"I'm sorry I said you weren't the least bit funny."

"It's okay, sir."

"I deeply regret saying you were a dumb kid, an idiot, a moron with the brains of a pile of mud."

"You never said that last part, Mr. President."

"Oh, I guess I was just thinking it. But I take it all back now. Funny Boy, you are our last and only hope.

Our nation turns to you in its hour of need. Will you help us?"

---

**SUGGESTION TO READER: As you read the following, have a friend hum "America the Beautiful" in the background.**

---

As I stood there on the podium in the White House, I gazed out at all the pleading faces before me. I thought about all the things I had come to love about my adopted planet. Things I had come to take for granted. Things like double coupons at the super-market. And intermittent windshield wipers. Those little yellow sticky notes that come in so handy.

I decided that it was up to me to make the world safe. Safe for Personal Pan Pizzas and Blow Pops and Groundhog Day. Safe for drive-through windows at fast-food restaurants. Safe for Ritz Bits and synchro-nized swimming. Safe for people who call you on the phone at dinnertime trying to sell you things. I felt tears welling up in my eyes.

"I'll *do* it!"

---

**NOTE TO READER: If you are reading this book in school, begin making noises like a chicken at this time. Maybe your teacher will think you are crazy and send you home for the day.**

## CHAPTER 13

---

# READ THIS CHAPTER! THIS IS WHEN IT GETS REALLY EXCITING AND IT LOOKS LIKE FUNNY BOY IS GOING TO DIE!

I, Funny Boy, was on my way for a final confrontation with the chitchatting cheeses from Chattanooga.

United States Government planes, helicopters, and cars rushed Bob Foster, Punch, and me to the Wisconsin barn where the cheeses were still headquartered. I had thrown away my copy of *Milton Berle's Private Joke File* and surfed the Internet looking for jokes and riddles. Armed with a full arsenal, we marched through the doors. We were immediately hit with a powerfully foul odor.

"Whew!" I choked. "Who cut the cheese?"

"Aha!" Mozzarella proclaimed. "I see our young friend Dummy Boy is here. We've been expecting you."

"That's *Funny* Boy," I announced, holding my nose. "I have been sent by the President of the United States to defend the planet Earth, including Antarctica, where nobody in their right mind would even want to go. Who's the big cheese around here?"

"I am," all the cheeses replied.

"You already used that joke once in this book," Punch whispered.

"I know," I replied. "But nobody laughed the first time, so I thought I would try again."

"Come to me, Funny Boy," Monterey Jack ordered. "I want to tell you something before we kill you."

Slowly, I approached the cheese.

"I'm not going to beat around the bush," Monterey Jack warned ominously. "You're getting too big for your britches, Funny Boy. This time you bit off more than you can chew. We are armed to the teeth. Actions speak louder than words. It is time for you to face the music. You may think you are funny, but we will have the last laugh. And that's the bottom line."

"Do you always have to talk in clichés?" I asked.

"Old customs die hard," Jack replied.

"Didn't you ever hear the cliché 'live and let live'?"

"That's easier said than done, Funny Boy."

"Look, I'll make a deal with you. Surrender now and we'll build a cheese-themed amusement park in Orlando, Florida."

"Hahahahaha!" Mozzarella cackled. "In twenty-four hours, your entire planet will be our *personal* amusement park!"

"Hmmm. Good point," I admitted. "Okay, then you asked for it. The time has come for me to tell jokes that are so funny you will die laughing."

"Don't count your chickens before they're hatched," Monterey Jack replied.

Suddenly, a long, low buzzing sound was heard. It lasted about five seconds.

"What was that?" Bob Foster asked.

"We have just turned on our invisible joke-deflector shield," Fontina snickered. "It is totally impenetrable to humor. Your jokes will just bounce off harmlessly. Hahahaha!"

"Joke-deflector shield?" Bob Foster repeated. "That's impossible."

"Go ahead and see for yourself," Mozzarella challenged. "Try a joke."

"Okay," I answered. "Where does a one-armed man do his shopping?"

"Where?" Punch asked.

"In a secondhand store."

The cheeses had no reaction at all.

"We didn't even hear it," Fontina hissed. "The joke bounced right off the shield."

"Try another one," Bob Foster suggested.

"Okay. Why were the little strawberries so upset?" I asked.

"Why?"

"Their parents were in a jam."

The cheeses just sat there, like cheeses.

"Drat!" I complained. "The joke-deflector shield is too strong. My jokes aren't going over."

"Did it ever occur to you that maybe they're just not funny?" Punch asked.

"Enough lame attempts at humor!" Romano shrieked.

Monterey Jack yelled, "Now it is time to separate the men from the boys!"

"Huh?"

"I think he means he's going to kill us," Bob Foster told me.

The four cheeses surrounded Bob Foster, Punch, and me, pushing us through a doorway and into a tiny room just big enough for the three of us. Once we were inside, the door shut behind us. The only furniture in the room was a chair.

"Help!" I yelled.

"You're in a pickle, Funny Boy!" Monterey Jack hollered through the door. "You don't have a ghost of a chance. Pack it in. The writing is on the wall."

I looked around. The walls were a pleasant off-white, with blue trim but no writing.

"What are you going to do with us?" hollered Bob Foster.

"Here's some food for thought, Funny Boy!"

Suddenly, a spray of creamy yellow goop shot out of a pipe on the ceiling.

It splattered over all of us.

"What's that stuff?" Punch asked. Bob Foster dipped a finger into the yellow goop and tasted it.

"It's Cheez Whiz!" he reported.

"That's right," Mozzarella shouted from outside.

"We will fill the room with Cheez Whiz until you are all dead! This is what we are going to do to Earth! Enjoy the rest of your life, Funny Boy! What's left of it! Haha-hahahahaha!"

The Cheez Whiz had coated the floor, and the level was now rising above our ankles. My feet were stuck in it. The cheese kept squirting out of the pipe, rising higher and higher.

"We're doomed!" Bob Foster moaned. "If the cheese reaches the ceiling, there will be no air left."

"We're going to drown in cheese!" Punch wailed. "What a horrible way to die!"

So, how are you enjoying the story so far? Exciting, isn't it? Do you think Funny Boy can escape from these cliché-cracking cheeses? Or is it all over for him? Will the President do anything to save him? What about Punch? Will she ever be able to get the Cheez Whiz out of her fur? Will Bob Foster still have cheese as a hobby, or will he get a life? Will Monterey Jack ever run out of clichés?

Okay, okay, back to the story . . .

## CHAPTER 14

# THE BIG SURPRISE ENDING THAT WILL COMPLETELY SHOCK YOU, UNLESS YOU ALREADY GUESSED IT.

The tiny room was almost completely filled with Cheez Whiz. Bob Foster and I climbed up on the chair so we could breathe the little air that was remaining at the top. Poor Punch was covered with cheese. I held her above my head. "We're goners!" Bob Foster shouted, spitting Cheez Whiz. "There's no way out!"

The level of Cheez Whiz kept rising. I was standing on my tiptoes to keep my nose out of it. A few more seconds and it would be over my head.

Suddenly, a loud bang was heard. The Cheez Whiz stopped rising and quickly began to drop. I could see that the door had been opened. The Cheez Whiz flowed out the opening like lava from a volcano. And standing there at the door was . . .

---

**You're just dying to know who it is, aren't you?**

---

And standing there at the door was . . . Tupper Camembert!

"Tupper!" I shouted. "What are *you* doing here?"

"Saving your life, my darling!"

"Huh?"

"I saw you on TV at that press conference," she explained. "You were so brave, so manly. Instantly I fell in love, hopelessly in love."

Bob Foster, Punch, and I stumbled out of the cheesy room, the Cheez Whiz dripping off us.

"But how did you get in here?" Bob Foster asked. "How did you get past those four giant cheeses?"

"See for yourself," Tupper grinned, motioning to the side.

Behind her were four gigantic plastic containers. Trapped inside them were Monterey Jack, Fontina, Romano, and Mozzarella.

"Tupperware!" Tupper announced proudly.

"Of course!" Bob Foster exclaimed. "Tupperware is the perfect container for storing just about any kind of leftovers! And they're dishwasher safe, too! Why didn't I think of it sooner?"

"You see," Tupper continued, "my great-great-grandfather was Earl S. Tupper, the inventor of Tupperware. I was named after him. I can get Tupperware in any size or shape that I want."

"That is the lamest explanation for a rescue I have ever heard," Punch said, shaking her head.

"Actually, I think the explanation in the second Funny Boy was even more lame than this one," declared Bob Foster.

"Hold your horses!" Monterey Jack hollered from inside his Tupperware prison. "Can't we bury the hatchet, clear the air? We have no ax to grind. It was all much ado about nothing."

I strolled over to Monterey Jack. "So," I gloated. "Now the glove is on the other hand!"

"You mean the shoe is on the other foot," Monterey Jack moaned.

"Right. I was never very good with clichés," I admitted. "You know, Monterey, this Tupperware you're in is microwavable. . . ."

"No!" the cheeses shrieked.

"Forget about microwaves," Tupper suggested. "I disabled the joke deflector. Why don't you just tell some of those funny jokes of yours?"

"You really think my jokes are funny, Tupper?"

"Hysterical!" Tupper exclaimed. "Won't you tell those cheeses some jokes and save the world . . . for me?"

"I'd rather be microwaved," Mozzarella moaned.

"For you, Tupper, anything. Okay you cheeses, how much did the pirate pay to get his ears pierced?"

"How much?"

"A buck an ear. Get it? A buccaneer?"

"Please stop!" Romano groaned. "It's bad enough that we have been confined in these Tupperware containers. Must we also listen to your pathetic attempts at humor?"

"Yes! Why couldn't they play cards on Noah's ark?"

"Why?"

"Because Noah sat on the deck."

"No more jokes. Please!" shouted Fontina. "The pain! The pain!"

"What's yellow and green and eats grass?" I asked.

"What?"

"A yellow-and-green grass eater. What's yellow and blue and eats grass?"

"A yellow-and-blue grass eater?" Mozzarella guessed.

"No," I informed him. "They only come in yellow and green."

"Stop the torture!" Romano begged. "Have you no sense of decency! In heaven's name, please stop this torture!"

"My sense of humor is beginning to *grate* on you, isn't it?" I sneered. "Get it? *Grate* on you?"

"Not puns!" Mozzarella screamed. "I'm begging you. Anything but puns!"

"Do you know where the first doughnut was made?"

"Where?"

"In Greece."

That was it. Suddenly, all four cheeses began to shrivel up. Their faces disappeared into themselves, leaving a big gloppy mess. All was quiet. I went over to Monterey Jack to see if he was still breathing.

"He's dead," I told the others. "Dead as a doornail."

We had a brief moment of silence to think about what had happened, and what could have happened if Tupper Camembert had not come along and rescued us.

"Well," Bob Foster finally said. "That's the way the cookie crumbles."

"The bigger they come, the harder they fall," Punch grinned.

"You live and learn," added Tupper.

"Some folks just can't take a joke," I concluded. "Okay, enough clichés." I wrapped my cheesy arms around Tupper Camembert and gave her a big hug.

"My hero!" She swooned.

Once again the forces of funniness had thwarted evil. I not only saved the world and conquered the forces of evil but I even got the girl. I was like the James Bond of kids!

Once again, I had made the world safe. Safe for mint-flavored dental floss and supermodels. Safe for inflatable furniture and battery-operated candy dispensers. Safe for the windchill factor and for movies based on thirty-year-old TV sitcoms that weren't even good thirty years ago.

That concludes this adventure. Until we meet again, my friends, let me leave you with two small pieces of wisdom. First, always remember that you are unique, just like everyone else. Second, if at first you don't succeed, skydiving is definitely not for you.

# A Biography of Dan Gutman

Dan Gutman was born in a log cabin in Illinois and used to write by candlelight with a piece of chalk on a shovel. Oh, wait a minute, that was Abraham Lincoln. Actually, Dan Gutman grew up in New Jersey and, for some reason, still lives there.

Somehow, Dan survived his bland and uneventful childhood, and then attended Rutgers University, where he majored in psychology for reasons he can't explain. After a few years of graduate studies, he disappointed his mother by moving to New York City to become a starving writer.

In the 1980s, after several penniless years writing untrue newspaper articles, unread magazine articles, and unsold screenplays, Gutman supported himself by writing about video games and selling unnecessary body parts. He edited *Video Games Player* magazine for four years. And, although he knew virtually nothing about computers, he spent the late 1980s writing a syndicated column on the subject.

In 1990, Gutman got the opportunity to write about something that had interested him since childhood: baseball. Beginning with *It Ain't Cheatin' If You Don't Get Caught* (1990), Gutman wrote several nonfiction books about the sport, covering subjects such as the game's greatest scandals and the history of its equipment.

The birth of his son, Sam, inspired Gutman to write for kids, beginning with *Baseball's Biggest Bloopers* (1993). In 1996, Gutman published *The Kid Who Ran for President*, a runaway hit about a twelve-year-old who (duh!) runs for president. He also continued writing about baseball, and the following year published *Honus & Me*, a story about a young boy who finds a rare baseball card that magically takes him back to 1909 to play with Honus Wagner, one of the game's early greats. This title stemmed a series about time-travel encounters with other baseball stars such as

Jackie Robinson, Babe Ruth, and, in *Ted & Me* (2012), Ted Williams.

In his insatiable quest for world domination, Dan also wrote *Miss Daisy Is Crazy* (2004) and launched the My Weird School series, which now spans more than forty books, most recently *Mayor Hubble Is in Trouble!* (2012).

As if he didn't have enough work to do, Gutman published *Mission Unstoppable* (2011), the first adventure novel in the Genius Files series, starring fraternal twins Coke and Pepsi McDonald. There will be six books in the series, in which the twins are terrorized by lunatic assassins while traveling cross-country during their summer vacation. These books are totally inappropriate for children, or anybody else for that matter.

Gutman lives in Haddonfield, New Jersey, with his wife and two children. But please don't stalk him.

Gutman and his sister Lucy in New York in 1956.

A young, stylish Gutman at home in Newark, New Jersey.

Gutman in his Little League uniform in 1968.

Gutman with two babies born in 1990:
the first baseball book he wrote, and his son, Sam.

Gutman in Liverpool, England, at the site of the real Strawberry Field.
"I idolize the Beatles and they inspire all my books," he says.

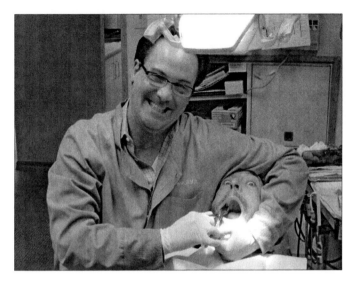

Gutman and his dentist at play (we hope).

Gutman in the midst of adoring fans at
Anderson's Bookshop in Naperville, Illinois.

When he's not writing, Gutman's busy with his favorite hobby, biking.

Gutman and his wife, Nina, at the spot where they met in 1982.

Gutman's wife, Nina, with their children, Sam and Emma.

"After thirty years I made the *New York Times* bestseller list," says Gutman, posing with the second book of the Genius Files, his hit series.

Visit the author at www.dangutman.com and www.openroadmedia.com/dangutman.

# EBOOKS BY DAN GUTMAN

## FROM OPEN ROAD MEDIA

Available wherever ebooks are sold

OPEN (11) ROAD

INTEGRATED MEDIA

**Open Road Integrated Media** is a digital publisher and multimedia content company. Open Road creates connections between authors and their audiences by marketing its ebooks through a new proprietary online platform, which uses premium video content and social media.

## Videos, Archival Documents, and New Releases

Sign up for the Open Road Media newsletter and get news delivered straight to your inbox.

Sign up now at
www.openroadmedia.com/newsletters

FIND OUT MORE AT
WWW.OPENROADMEDIA.COM

FOLLOW US:
**@openroadmedia** and
**Facebook.com/OpenRoadMedia**

CPSIA information can be obtained at www.ICGtesting.com
Printed in the USA
BVOW040927140313

315506BV00003B/3/P